This book belongs to:

....

....

Editor: Ruth Symons
Designer: Anya Paul
Editorial Director: Victoria Garrard
Art Director: Laura Roberts-Jensen

Copyright © QED Publishing 2015

First published in the UK in 2015 by
QED Publishing
A Quarto Group company
The Old Brewery
6 Blundell Street
London
N7 9BH

www.qed-publishing.co.uk

A catalogue record for this book is available from the British Library.

ISBN 978 1 78171 761 5

Printed in China

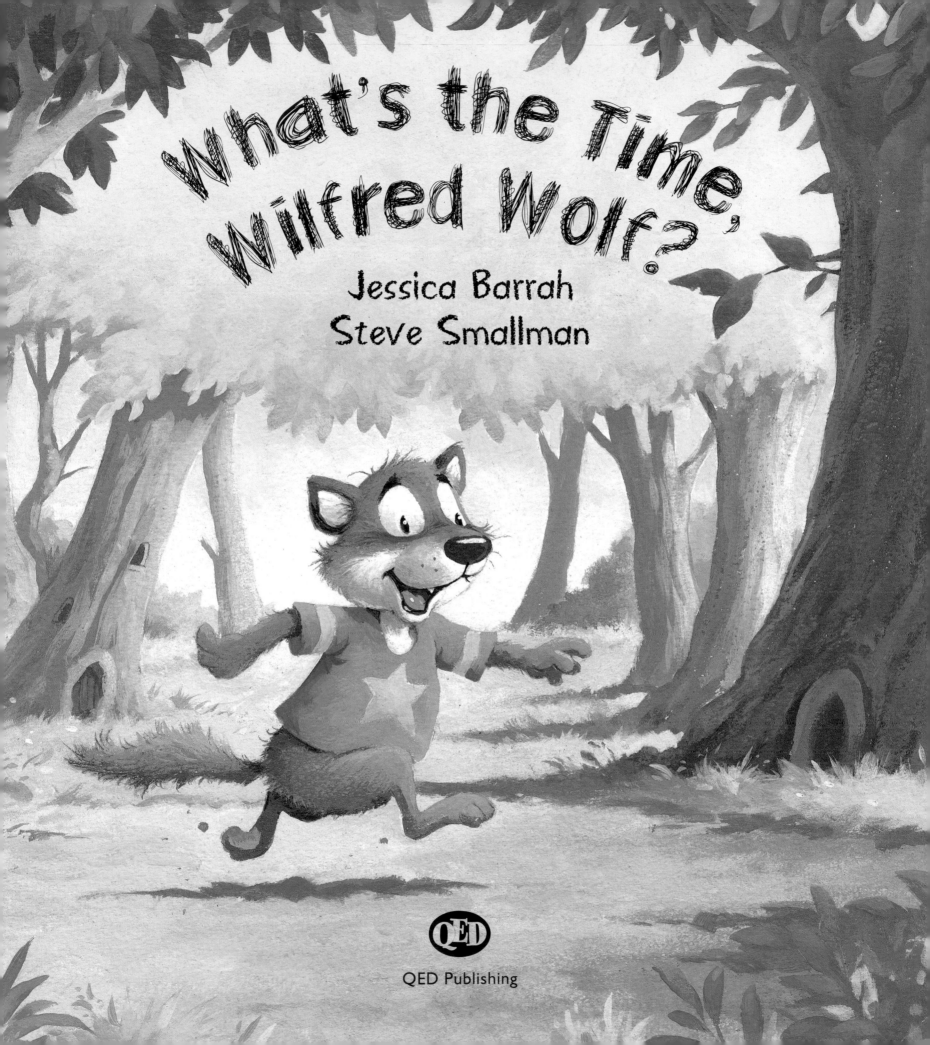

What's the Time, Wilfred Wolf?

Jessica Barrah

Steve Smallman

QED Publishing

Wilfred Wolf couldn't tell the time. Big hands and little hands were too confusing.

He just ate and slept when he felt like it – which was quite often.

One morning, a party invitation arrived.

Dear Wilfred,
Please come to my party at 3 o'clock tomorrow.
Love, Ella

"Yippee! A party! But how will I know the right time to go?" yelped Wilfred.

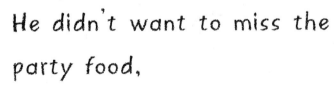

He didn't want to miss the party food,

or the dancing,

or the games.

Maybe his friend Boris Bear could help.

"Don't worry, Wilfred," said Boris.

"Take this cuckoo clock. Every hour a little
bird pops out and says, 'cuckoo!'.
Three 'cuckoos' means three o'clock."

Cuckoo!   Cuckoo!   Cuckoo!

Wilfred went home and put the clock on the table.

He waited...

...and waited...

...and waited.

After a while, Wilfred felt hungry. His tummy told him it must be about time for lunch.

Rumble
Rumble

Just as Wilfred started eating,
the cuckoo sprang out of its clock.

CUCKOO!

"WAH!"

screamed Wilfred, flinging his fork.

POING! went the fork.

SPLAT! went the sausage and mash.

SMASH! went the clock.

What a shock for Wilfred!

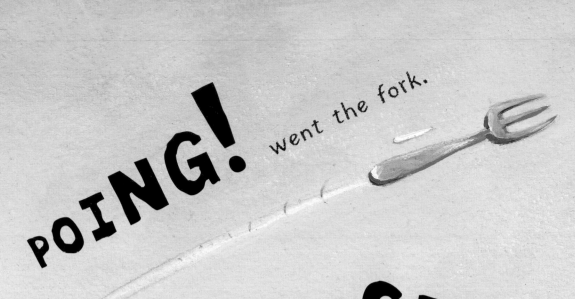

Wilfred went to ask his friend Amelia Squirrel for help.

"Don't worry, Wilfred, you can borrow my watch," said Amelia. "It has numbers, but no hands."

"Fantastic," said Wilfred.

Wilfred went home and made a birthday card for Ella.

He got all sticky with glitter and glue, so he took a bath.

Then he checked the time. **"oh no!"** Wilfred cried. All the numbers had disappeared!

Wilfred went outside
and howled.

"What's the matter with **you-hoo-hoo?"** said Oscar Owl, flying by.

Wilfred told him about the watch.

"Oh, Wilfred," said Oscar. "Watches don't like getting wet. But I can tell the time. I'll hoot down your chimney at 3 o'clock." "Oh, thank you, Oscar," said Wilfred.

Wilfred got dressed for the party and waited for Oscar.

At last it was time to go!

Wilfred walked through the forest, over the
bridge and around the hill to Ella's house.

He knocked on the door. Where was everyone?
It was very quiet.

"What are you doing here?" said Ella.

"I'm here for the party!" said Wilfred.
"Oscar Owl said it was time to go."

"Oh, Wilfred," said Ella. "Owls are
only awake at night. It's
3 o'clock in the morning now!
The party's not until 3 o'clock
this afternoon."

Wilfred walked back home, feeling tired and confused. On the way, he met Henry Cockerel.

"Henry, could you let me know when it's 3 o'clock this afternoon?" Wilfred asked.

"No can **cockadoodle-do**," said Henry.
"I only wake everyone up in the morning."

Wilfred slept all morning. He slept through lunchtime, and into the afternoon.

He only woke up when there was
a **knock** at his door.

"Hello, Wilfred," said Albert Mouse.
"Aren't you going to Ella's party?"

"I can't tell the time," said Wilfred, sadly,
"so I don't know when to go."

"We can tell the time!" said little Benjamin Mouse.
"We'll teach you!" said Lily Mouse.

"This is the clock face," said Lily, drawing a big chalk clock on the ground. "Albert's the big hand. When he points straight up at the 12, that means it's the beginning of the hour."

"And Lily's the little hand," said Albert. "When she points to the 2, that means it's 2 o'clock."

6 o'clock!

4 o'clock!

3 o'clock!

3 o'clock – it's party time!

Wilfred had a wonderful time at the party. He ate lots of party food and danced with all his friends.

And he knew when it
was time to go home...

NEXT STEPS

Show the children the cover again. Did the children guess what the story would be about from the picture or the title of the story?

Wilfred can't tell the time at first, but he knows when to eat and sleep. Ask the children what time they usually wake up, eat meals and go to bed. Is it different at weekends?

Ask the children if they can tell the time. Are there any other ways of knowing what time it is?

Wilfred is worried about being late to the party. Ask the children if they have ever been late for something? What happened? Why can it be important to arrive on time?

Oscar Owl is awake at night, and sleeps in the day. Ask if the children know anyone who works at night? What kind of work might people do at night?

Wilfred loves parties. Ask the children to draw a picture of the best party ever! It could show the children with their friends and family, or with the animals from the story.

Play the game "What's the time, Mr Wolf?".
One child is Mr Wolf and stands with their back to the others. The group asks, "What's the time, Mr Wolf?" If Mr Wolf answers "3 o'clock", the children must each take three steps forwards.
If Mr Wolf answers "dinner time", he or she will turn and try to catch another player. Whoever is caught becomes the new Mr Wolf.